OUT OF BOUNDS

Check out these other L'il D books!

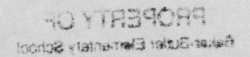

Hey L'il D!
OUT OF BOUNDS

By Bob Lanier
and Heather Goodyear

Illustrated by
Desire Grover

A
LITTLE APPLE
PAPERBACK

SCHOLASTIC INC.

New York   Toronto   London   Auckland   Sydney
Mexico City   New Delhi   Hong Kong   Buenos Aires

I'd like to dedicate this book to all the wonderful teachers and counselors at P. S. 74 whose passion for education shown brightly and made learning fun.
— B. L.

To Emily, Joseph, and Abigail — I love every day and every adventure with you.
— H. G.

ISBN 0-439-40902-0

12 11 10 9 8 7 6 5 4 3 2   3 4 5 6 7 8/0

Printed in the U.S.A.   40
First printing, June 2003

Dear Reader,

Thank you for picking up this book. It's all about when I was a kid — back when people called me L'il Dobber, instead of Big Bob. Back before I played in the NBA.

I grew up in Buffalo, New York. I loved basketball and played every chance I got. Luckily, I had great friends to hang out with both on and off the court. We had a lot of fun adventures — and they're all included in these books.

Soon you'll meet me as a kid (remember, they call me L'il Dobber!). You'll also meet my friends Joe, Sam, and Gan. We are always up to something! We may not do the right thing all the time, but whatever we do, we learn from it. And we have a lot of fun!

And that's something I hope you do with this HEY L'IL D! book — have fun. Because believe me, reading is one of the most fun, most important things that you can do.

I hope you like my story.

Bob Lanier

Contents

Chapter 1
The Grouch

L'il Dobber and his friends Joe and Gan stretched out along Northland Avenue, carrying plastic bags. They were hard at work on their leaf-collecting assignment.

"Here's an elm tree!" called Sam, Joe's twin sister. They ran to join her and add another leaf to their bags.

Sam was in a different fourth grade class than the boys, but she had tagged along anyway. She liked to be included in any adventure — big or small. Even if the adventure was actually homework.

They made their way down the street to the Laniers' brick house.

Sam scooped up an armful of the red leaves covering L'il Dobber's front lawn. "Hey, Joe, I think our hair is the same color as these red maple leaves," she said. Sam threw the armful of leaves over her brother's head. "See?" she laughed.

That started it. Soon the four friends were in an all-out leaf battle, tossing heaping handfuls all over each other.

L'il Dobber's older sister, Geraldine, stuck her head out the Laniers' front door.

"Hey, L'il D! Mom said five minutes until dinner!" she yelled and disappeared back into the house.

"Truce!" called L'il Dobber.

The battle ended.

"We still have to find one more kind of leaf," said Joe, pulling a red maple leaf from the hood of his jacket.

"What have you got so far?" asked Sam.

They searched for their bags under the piles of leaves they'd thrown.

"Here's mine!" L'il Dobber picked up his bag. "Birch, elm, ash, and red maple," he said.

Gan pointed to the yard next door. "I think that's a sugar maple."

They peered over at the tall tree standing in the perfectly mowed lawn.

"It looks like the pictures we studied in class," said Joe.

L'il Dobber shook his head at his friends. "You all *know* we can't go over there," he told them. "Are there any others?"

They scanned the trees up and down either side of the street.

"I can't believe no one else has a sugar maple," said Gan. "It's the state tree of New York."

Sam flopped down onto a pile of leaves. "Too bad the only one is in Mr. Palmer's yard," she said.

L'il Dobber picked up a leaf, tossed it in the air, and watched it float to the ground.

"There's no way I'm taking any leaves off the Grouch's tree," he said. "The Grouch" was the name local kids had for his neighbor, Mr. Palmer.

"But the leaves are just on the *ground*," Joe pointed out. "Not on the *tree*."

L'il Dobber shook his head. "No way. He keeps his grass so neat, he'll see our footprints if we step on it," he said. "Then he'll run out of his house yelling at us."

"I think we could reach some from the sidewalk," Gan said, studying the yard next door. "Just lean over the fence."

L'il Dobber glanced at his front door, knowing he only had a few minutes left. Then he looked at the small house next door.

"OK, let's try," L'il Dobber said, turning to his friends. "But just reach from the sidewalk."

"I don't need one, so I'm going to stay here," Sam said from her bed of leaves. "I'm not going near the Grouch's house if I don't have to."

The boys took long, slow strides along the sidewalk toward the sugar maple tree.

Crackle. "Shhh!"

Crackle. "Shhh!"

Each time one of the boys stepped on a leaf, Sam called out, "Shhh!"

Crackle. "Shhh!"

They all turned around and hissed, "Shhh!" back at her. She was making them even more nervous with all of her shushing.

L'il Dobber, Joe, and Gan reached the ground beneath the tree. Each one bent carefully over the fence to pick up a leaf from the edge of the grass.

Just as L'il Dobber was putting a leaf in his bag, Mr. Palmer's screen door burst open. L'il Dobber jolted upright and saw Mr. Palmer

standing on his front steps with his fists on his hips. He was dressed in his usual old jeans and untucked flannel shirt. His wild angry eyes matched his wild gray hair.

"What are you kids doing?" shouted Mr. Palmer.

L'il Dobber never knew what to say to his neighbor. Joe and Gan, whose hands were shaking as they held their leaves, were having the same problem.

"Bob Lanier!" Mr. Palmer shouted at L'il Dobber. "I asked you a question."

Almost everybody called Bob Lanier by his nickname — L'il Dobber. But Mr. Palmer was not like everybody. In fact, he wasn't like *anybody*.

L'il Dobber coughed. "C-c-collecting leaves. Um, it's for school. Homework," he stammered, trying to explain.

"You tell your teacher to give you home-work that keeps you out of my yard." Mr. Palmer turned and slammed his screen door shut behind him.

L'il Dobber, Joe, and Gan sprinted back toward the safety of L'il Dobber's yard.

Sam jumped up to join Joe and Gan who kept running full speed down the street. L'il Dobber ran straight inside for dinner. No one wanted to stop — in case Mr. Palmer returned.

Chapter 2
Squish

Lunch recess was the four friends' favorite part of the school day. It meant free time to do what they loved most — play basketball.

Traffic whooshed by outside the fence. Jump ropes twirled. Hopscotchers jumped. But L'il Dobber, Joe, Gan, and Sam barely noticed any of it as they jogged to the school yard court to shoot some hoops.

L'il Dobber set his basketball down under the basket while they kicked away the leaves that had fallen on the small cement area. When they'd cleared the court, Gan picked up L'il Dobber's basketball and tossed it to Joe.

"How about Joe and me against Gan and Sam today?" asked L'il Dobber.

"OK. You start, Joe," said Gan and went up to guard him.

Thud, thud, thud. Joe stood at the top of the key, pumping his arm up and down, trying hard to dribble the basketball. It wouldn't bounce any higher than his knee.

"Man, my arm is going to be sore this afternoon," said Joe. "Your ball won't dribble, L'il Dobber."

"It felt squishy when I threw it to Joe," remarked Gan.

"Let me see," said L'il Dobber.

Joe tossed the ball to L'il Dobber and he squeezed it between his hands. "I can't get it to hold any air," L'il Dobber complained. "I filled it up yesterday afternoon and this morning. It keeps deflating."

"Maybe it's got a little hole," Sam suggested.

"You should put it in the bathtub after school," said Gan.

L'il Dobber clutched the smushy basketball to his chest. "Why would I do that?" he asked.

"Because under water, air will bubble out of the hole," Gan answered.

"Really?" Joe asked Gan. "Are you sure?"

"Yeah," said Gan. "And then you can tape the hole if there is one."

"Cool," said L'il Dobber. He tried to roll the lopsided ball around in his hands. "What should we do until then?" he asked.

"I guess we can't play two-on-two today," said Gan.

"And we can't drive for any layups because we can't dribble," Sam pointed out.

"Which means we can't practice spin

moves, either," added L'il Dobber. "What's left?"

"I guess we'll practice a lot of foul shots today," said Joe. He stepped up to the faintly painted foul line. "Give me the ball, L'il D."

L'il Dobber handed Joe the basketball and joined Gan and Sam under the basket.

Joe aimed from the foul line and shot the ball. It hit the right side of the backboard and dropped straight to the ground. "It's like throwing a rock," he said.

Sam grabbed the ball and tried a jump shot. The ball folded over the edge of the rim and then fell through the hoop.

Gan took the ball and headed to the foul line. "Let me try," he said. He aimed and threw the squishy ball into the air. They all watched it smack the top of the board and slide slowly down into the basket.

For the rest of recess, they kept trying to shoot and rebound. But the quickly deflating ball squished more and more with each drop from the backboard.

Chapter 3
Surgery

On his walk home from school that afternoon, L'il Dobber reached the front of his house and stopped short. Oh, no! Mr. Palmer's perfect yard was *covered* with newspapers!

Where did all those newspapers come from? he wondered.

L'il Dobber stood perfectly still and watched Mr. Palmer bending down to grab the papers and wad them up. Suddenly, Mr. Palmer looked up, and L'il Dobber got caught staring.

"Did you and your friends do this?" demanded Mr. Palmer.

L'il Dobber was so surprised that he

couldn't speak. Finally he managed to blurt out, "N-no."

"I'm not so sure," said Mr. Palmer, narrowing his gray eyes at L'il Dobber.

"We didn't throw those papers in your yard," L'il Dobber insisted.

"Hmpf," grunted Mr. Palmer. He turned away and kept cleaning.

L'il Dobber slumped into his house. He was disappointed and a little angry that Mr. Palmer didn't believe him.

Later that afternoon, after dunking his basketball in the bathtub, L'il Dobber found his mom and sister reading in the living room.

"Look at my ball," he said sadly. He held up his flat basketball. It was covered with the four largest Band-Aids he'd been able to find.

"What happened?" asked his mom in surprise.

"Did a doctor do surgery on it?" joked Geraldine over the top of her book.

L'il Dobber glared at her.

"How long until it's feeling better?" she continued joking in a baby voice.

L'il Dobber ignored her and turned to his mom. "It has holes. Can we go buy me a new one?"

Mrs. Lanier shook her head. "We can't afford to just go out and buy a basketball right now, Bobby," she said.

"You don't get new toys just 'cause you break one," Geraldine said in the snotty grown-up voice that bothered L'il Dobber even more than her baby voice.

"My basketball isn't a *toy*!" he said. "Teddy bears and dolls are toys — I *need* my basketball."

"Whatever," answered Geraldine. She grabbed her book and stood up from the chair where she had been reading. As she brushed by L'il Dobber, she whispered, "Some kids carry around a teddy bear or doll, you carry around a basketball. Same thing."

Normally, L'il Dobber would have had a

comeback for his sister, but she was already out the door. Besides, he had bigger worries right now.

He turned the bandaged ball over and over in his hands. "What should I do, Mom?" he asked.

"You can use the money you have saved to buy a new one," answered Mrs. Lanier.

"But I don't have any money," he answered.

His mom pushed her hair back from her

face. "What about your allowance?" she asked him.

He flopped down in the chair where Geraldine had been. "I spent what I had saved on that lockbox to keep my money in," he said. "The problem is, now I don't have any money to put in it."

"Well, then you'll need to start saving again, Bobby," said his mother.

"Are you sure we can't go buy me one?" L'il Dobber asked.

"Yes, I'm sure," she answered. Mrs. Lanier opened her book as if to start reading, but then paused and looked up. "Very sure," she added.

L'il Dobber looked at his bandaged ball and thought of his father. Dit, as he called his dad, shared his love of basketball. Back in high school, Dit's friends had called him "Big Dobber" on the basketball court, and the nickname stuck. Since L'il Dobber wanted to be a basketball star just like his dad, people called him "L'il Dobber."

"Will Dit be home soon?" L'il Dobber asked his mom.

She glanced up from her book. "You and I both know that your dad likes basketball as much as you do, Bobby. But we also know that he is going to tell you the same thing I did."

"Save my money?" asked L'il Dobber.

His mom nodded. "That's right." She smiled, but her answer was firm.

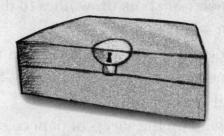

Chapter 4
A Two-dollar Start

After dinner, L'il Dobber sat on the beige-carpeted floor of his bedroom, surrounded by paper, tape, scissors, and markers. His dad walked in to find L'il Dobber taping sheets of white paper together.

"Is this a project for school?" he asked.

L'il Dobber concentrated on taping the last two sheets together evenly, and then held up the long line of paper for Dit to see. "This is my savings chart," he announced.

L'il Dobber drew a square backboard and basket on the top sheet. Then, with a black marker, he drew two long lines down the rest of the taped sheets to make the basketball pole. Next, he drew lines to divide the pole into sections.

"I looked in the newspaper ads and saw a new basketball that costs twenty-five dollars," L'il Dobber said.

He held up the sheets of paper again. "I'll color in a section on the pole for each dollar I earn," he explained. "When I color in the last section and reach the basket, I'll have twenty-five dollars. Enough for my new basketball."

Dit smiled at L'il Dobber. "That's quite a system," Dit said. "I'm very proud of you."

L'il Dobber smiled back. It always felt good when his dad was proud of him.

"I came to tell you that your mom and I want to give you two dollars to get you started," said Dit. He held out two dollar bills.

"Thanks!" L'il Dobber exclaimed with an even bigger smile. He took the money and set it on his desk to put in his lockbox as soon as he finished his chart.

"This is great. I can color in the first two sections right away," he said.

Dit nodded. Then he saw the bandage-covered basketball on L'il Dobber's bed and started to laugh.

"I tried to fix the holes I told you about at dinner," L'il Dobber said quietly.

Dit could see by the look on L'il Dobber's face how upset he was about his broken basketball.

"Finish your chart," said Dit as he turned to leave L'il Dobber's bedroom, "then we'll go out to the garage and find some duct tape to fix up your ball."

"OK," agreed L'il Dobber. "Thanks, Dit." He grabbed a red and a blue marker, Detroit Pistons colors, and colored in the first two sections on his chart.

Chapter 5
Dribbling

The next day after school, L'il Dobber was dribbling up and down his driveway. Up to the garage with his right hand, down to the street with his left hand. The duct tape was holding pretty well.

He'd been up and down the driveway thirteen times without losing his dribble. He was going for twenty.

Up and down. Up and down.

On L'il Dobber's next trip up to the garage, Mr. Palmer slid open a side window on his house.

"Stop that noise!" he yelled, leaning out the window.

L'il Dobber jumped and the ball bounced away from his left hand.

"You've been up and down that driveway a hundred times," scolded Mr. Palmer from the window.

Only fifteen, thought L'il Dobber.

"Now stop bouncing that ball," demanded Mr. Palmer. "I'm trying to take a nap."

L'il Dobber picked up his ball from the side of the driveway and walked inside. Right before he slammed his back door shut, he heard Mr. Palmer slam his window shut.

"What's all that banging?" asked Mrs. Lanier over the basket of laundry she was carrying through the kitchen.

"Do you think the Grouch will move soon?" asked L'il Dobber.

"Bobby . . ." warned Mrs. Lanier on her way into the living room.

"Sorry, Mom," said L'il Dobber. His mom didn't like when he called their neighbor "the Grouch."

"Do you think *Mr. Palmer* will move soon?" he asked as he followed her through the living room and down the hallway of bed-rooms.

"Oh, I doubt it," his mom answered. She stopped in her bedroom and set the laundry basket on the bed. "He's lived there for years."

"I can't do *anything* with him next door," complained L'il Dobber.

His mom shrugged. "He's just not a very happy person."

"Why not?" asked L'il Dobber.

"You know, I'm not really sure," she answered thoughtfully, as she folded a blue T-shirt. "He doesn't seem to have any family or friends, though. Maybe he's lonely."

"Well, he's not going to make any friends acting like he does," L'il Dobber said.

"That's true," his mom agreed. "But since we live next door to him, we have to be as kind as we can be."

L'il Dobber's mom handed him one of the piles of clothes she had sorted. "How about putting these away in your room and then you can go see if Joe, Sam, and Gan want to

play ball at Delaware Park for a while before dinner," she suggested.

L'il Dobber grabbed the pile. "All right!" he agreed, instantly happier. He loved going to the local park with his friends. He hoped they were all free to play.

At the end of the week, Dit came into the kitchen while Geraldine and L'il Dobber were doing homework at the table.

Dit handed some money to Geraldine. "Here's your allowance for this week, Geri," he told her. "Good work on your chores."

"And here's yours, L'il Dobber," he said. L'il Dobber eagerly stretched out his hand. "Your usual two dollars. Plus three more for all the extra jobs you've done."

L'il Dobber's mom nodded and smiled at him as she walked into the kitchen.

Dit put the money in L'il Dobber's hand and said proudly, "Our yard is raked clean and my pickup truck looks mighty fine on the inside."

"And I haven't had to water the plants once this week," added his mom.

"What does that bring your total to?" Dit asked L'il Dobber.

"I think seven dollars," L'il Dobber said excitedly. "I'm going to check." He ran out of the kitchen.

In his bedroom, he picked up the lockbox key from his windowsill and reached for the box under his bed. He unlocked the box, placed his five-dollar earnings inside, and re-locked it. This time, he carefully put the key under his pillow and hid the lockbox in his second dresser drawer.

L'il Dobber thought his chart looked great hanging on the wall between two drawings he had done of his favorite basketball players' jerseys.

He grabbed purple and green markers from his desk, Milwaukee Bucks colors this time, and colored in the next five sections of the pole. He could almost feel the brand-new basketball in his hands!

Chapter 6
Broken Flowers

Monday after school, L'il Dobber was throwing his basketball against the side of his house and seeing how high it would bounce back to him. He had just pumped it full of air, and if he hit the base of the house just right the ball bounced so high he had to jump to catch it.

Shwip, shwip, shwip.

The sound of Mr. Palmer's hedge clippers floated over the fence from next door. L'il Dobber pictured him hacking away any branches that dared to stick out of his perfectly designed bushes.

L'il Dobber threw the ball hard at the base of his house.

"Hi, L'il D!" came a yell from the street. L'il Dobber turned to see Gan waving out of the van window as he drove past with his family.

L'il Dobber waved back, and the ball bounced over his head. It sailed through the air and disappeared into Mr. Palmer's front yard.

L'il Dobber sighed. "Uh-oh."

He crept across his driveway to the side of Mr. Palmer's house and peeked around the corner at the front yard. No basketball.

L'il Dobber carefully stuck his head out just a little farther and he saw his ball. Sitting right in the middle of the flowers it had crushed when it rolled over them.

The hedge clippers suddenly stopped.

"Uh-oh." L'il Dobber sighed again. Mr. Palmer had seen the ball, too.

L'il Dobber whipped his head back around the corner and flattened himself against the side wall of the house. He didn't know what to do.

Slowly, he tiptoed back across the driveway to his own house. He silently opened the back door and crept through. Then, just as silently, he closed the door behind him.

"Mom," L'il Dobber whispered.

His mom stood at the kitchen counter making chicken for dinner. She turned and gave him a puzzled look. "What?" she whispered back.

"My ball went into Mr. Palmer's yard," L'il Dobber said.

"Why are you whispering?" asked his mom, still whispering herself.

"So he won't hear me."

Mrs. Lanier smiled and said in a normal voice, "You're inside now. I don't think he can."

"Oh, yeah." L'il Dobber smiled, too. "So what should I do?"

"Go ask for your ball back."

"From the Grouch?" L'il Dobber asked in disbelief.

"Bobby . . ." L'il Dobber's mom scolded and shook a raw chicken leg at him.

"It also smashed some flowers," L'il Dobber admitted.

"Then you'd better apologize, too," said his mother. She turned on the water in the sink to start cleaning the chicken.

L'il Dobber could see his mom wasn't going to give him an idea that he would like any better, so he turned and trudged back out the door. He kept trudging all the way to his neighbor's front yard.

Mr. Palmer's bright green-and-yellow flannel shirt looked a lot happier than his face when he turned from picking up smashed flowers and saw L'il Dobber standing by the fence.

"I'm not giving your ball back," he told L'il Dobber right away.

L'il Dobber was so surprised that he forgot to be nervous and blurted out, "Why?!"

"Do you see what you did to my flowers?" Mr. Palmer growled and held up a bunch of flowers with broken stems.

"Yes," L'il Dobber said quietly. "And I came to apologize."

Mr. Palmer stared at him with his gray eyes. They made L'il Dobber very uneasy and suddenly, he was tongue-tied.

"Well, are you going to apologize?" Mr. Palmer asked.

"Yes, yes, I am," L'il Dobber stammered. "I'm sorry."

"I accept your apology," Mr. Palmer said

gruffly. "I need to put these in some water."
He took the crumpled flowers and walked up
his front steps.

Mr. Palmer had already pulled open the
screen door when L'il Dobber asked, "Can I
have my ball back now?"

"So you can ruin more of my flowers? I
don't think so," Mr. Palmer said and disappeared into his house.

L'il Dobber trudged back home. He

walked through the back door, into the kitchen, and past his mom who was dipping chicken in batter to be fried.

"What happened, Bobby?" she called after L'il Dobber.

"I need a new ball," he mumbled back sadly.

In his bedroom, L'il Dobber got his lockbox key from under the pencil cup on his desk. Then he dug around in the back left corner of his closet where he had hidden the box last night.

At his desk, he counted the money again. His savings was up to nine dollars.

But instead of feeling good that he had *already* saved nine out of twenty-five dollars, L'il Dobber felt miserable that he had *only* saved nine out of twenty-five dollars. Nine felt like a long way from twenty-five right now. Sixteen dollars away, in fact.

L'il Dobber hid the key behind his savings chart and put the lockbox behind his clothes hamper. Then he flung himself onto his bed. He laid on his back, angry at Mr.

Palmer, until his stomach started growling from the delicious smell filling the house.

Mr. Palmer might keep him away from his basketball, but he wasn't going to keep him away from fried chicken. L'il Dobber jumped up and headed toward the kitchen for dinner.

Chapter 7
Something's Missing

L'il Dobber, Joe, and Gan were on their way to school the next day when Gan asked, "Why does it seem so quiet?"

"Yeah," agreed Joe. "It's been bugging me, too."

They looked around. The usual noisy crowd of kids heading to school was the same. The busy traffic on Northland Avenue was the same.

"I don't know," said L'il Dobber. He was too sad about his basketball to care what it sounded like outside.

"Know what?" he asked Joe and Gan

miserably. "Mr. Palmer stole my ball yesterday."

"That's it!" Gan exclaimed.

"What's it?" asked L'il Dobber.

Gan pointed at his friend. "You're not dribbling your ball," he said.

"That *is* it," agreed Joe.

"What's it?" questioned L'il Dobber again.

"You've dribbled that ball on the way to school every day since I met you," said Gan.

Joe nodded in agreement. "I always hear 'step, bounce, step, bounce,' walking next to you."

Now that his friends had mentioned it, L'il Dobber also missed the noise of the ball smacking the cement.

"The Grouch is even ruining my walk to school," he muttered.

The next morning, L'il Dobber walked out his front door and nearly tripped over something on the porch. He and Geraldine looked down.

"My ball!" he yelled.

L'il Dobber picked up his basketball, tossed it high in the air, and caught it. Then he glanced next door. No sign of Mr. Palmer.

Geraldine bent down and picked up something else off the porch. "Here you go," she said, handing him a piece of paper.

"What's this?" asked L'il Dobber.

"It was under your basketball," she said.

L'il Dobber unfolded the sheet of paper.

The note said:

I was angry about my flowers. You can have
your ball back. Keep it out of my yard.

"Mr. Palmer says to keep it out of his yard," L'il Dobber told Geraldine.

"Well, I'm glad you got your favorite toy back," she teased him as they walked to the sidewalk.

"*I'm* surprised," said L'il Dobber. "I didn't think he could do anything nice."

"Me, either." Geraldine agreed. "See ya after school, L'il Dobber," she said and turned left to walk to middle school.

"See ya!" answered L'il Dobber and turned right.

Step, bounce, step, bounce — L'il Dobber tried to go back to his usual walk, even with a flat ball. After a few steps he looked back and saw Mr. Palmer coming down his driveway with a wheelbarrow.

"Thank you for giving me my ball back," L'il Dobber called to his neighbor.

Mr. Palmer looked up.

"Hmpf," he grunted and then looked away.

I guess he's back to being mean again, thought L'il Dobber. *At least I can tell my mom I tried to be kind.*

He happily tossed his ball in the air and hurried to meet Joe and Gan.

Chapter 8
Pop!

"Remember. My house in a half hour," L'il Dobber told Gan on the way home from school that afternoon.

"I'll be there," said Gan as he turned up his driveway.

L'il Dobber kept walking down the street. He passed the Stephenses' house and jumped when their big golden retriever barked from inside their front door. Next, he passed the Tanners' house and laughed at two squirrels fighting over an acorn. He was watching the winner run away with the acorn when he saw a flash of blue flannel up ahead. L'il Dobber quickly ducked behind the nearest tree.

Carefully, L'il Dobber peeked around the tree trunk. He waited until Mr. Palmer's back was to him, then sprinted past the Whitleys' and up his driveway.

Mrs. Lanier and Geraldine looked up when he came through the door.

"What's the big smile for, Bobby?" asked L'il Dobber's mom.

"This smile is because I just missed running into Mr. Palmer," L'il Dobber announced.

His mom frowned at him, so L'il Dobber quickly added, "*And*, I'm smiling because I found twenty-three cents on the way home. That makes fifty cents that I've found on the sidewalk!" Mrs. Lanier raised one eyebrow at him, but didn't say anything else.

A half hour later, L'il Dobber, Joe, Sam, and Gan stood in front of L'il Dobber's house tossing his basketball back and forth. L'il Dobber had given it a fresh bandaging of duct tape, and it was holding air pretty well. The cars on Northland Avenue made a little breeze as they sped by.

"Let's see how far apart we can bounce pass it," said Sam.

"Maybe we can make it all the way to Gan's house," said Joe.

"I don't know," said L'il Dobber. "That's five houses down."

"We can try," said Gan.

"We'll start close and then spread out," Sam instructed.

L'il Dobber and Sam stood on the sidewalk across from Joe and Gan. Sam held the

ball with two hands, stepped forward, and bounced it to Joe. He passed it to L'il Dobber. L'il Dobber bounced it to Gan. Gan passed it back to Sam.

"Now L'il Dobber and I will take a step backward," said Sam.

"Good passes, guys," said Gan after they had made it through another round.

L'il Dobber and Sam took another step back. "Here you go, Joe," Sam called to her brother.

Just as Sam bounced the ball, they heard Mr. Palmer's screen door creak open. The four friends looked at one another with panicked expressions, and then darted quickly across L'il Dobber's lawn. They dove over the steps and slid, face first, onto the porch.

"We made it!" Sam whispered happily. "He didn't see us!"

"Where's my ball?" L'il Dobber asked in a low voice.

Pop!

L'il Dobber whipped around to face the street. "Oh, no!" he gasped.

His basketball was being shoved along Northland Avenue as car after car bumped over it. L'il Dobber's heart sank lower into his stomach with each push of the ball.

"It must've rolled into the street when we ran," Joe said sadly.

"Sorry," said Gan.

"Yeah," Sam quietly agreed.

"It wouldn't have gotten run over if we didn't have to run away from Mr. Palmer," said L'il Dobber in an angry voice. "I hope he moves soon."

Gan almost jumped up in excitement. "Is he going to?" he asked.

"No," answered L'il Dobber. "I just keep hoping he will."

They lay hidden on the porch until Mr. Palmer finished watering his flowers. L'il Dobber spent the whole time peeking over the railing to keep a lookout.

When they were sure Mr. Palmer was back inside his house, Gan, Joe, and Sam snuck down the porch steps and ran home. L'il Dobber looked down the street, wondering if his ball was in the next city by now.

"Bobby! Dinner!" L'il Dobber heard his mom yell out the back door.

He walked off the porch and around the house. The smell met him as soon as he opened the door. Liver.

Tonight would *have to be liver,* thought L'il Dobber as he went to wash his hands. Then he slumped back to his chair at the kitchen table.

Usually, L'il Dobber liked anything his mom made — she was a great cook. But the one thing he couldn't stomach was liver. Maybe it was the horrible smell, or maybe it was because his mom tried to disguise it with gravy and rice. Any food that had to be disguised couldn't possibly be any good.

L'il Dobber ladled a tiny bit of gravy onto his plate from the pot in the center of the table and covered it with a mountain of rice. He scooped some of the smelly, runny sauce onto his spoon, tilted it, and watched it plop back onto his plate.

At least he could talk first tonight since the rest of the family had their mouths full of meat. "My ball got run over," he told them sadly.

"Run over?" asked his mom. "When?"

L'il Dobber told his parents and Geraldine what had just happened outside. "How am I going to earn the rest of the money for a new basketball?" he asked. "I need one — fast."

Dit took a big bite of liver, and L'il Dobber tried not to grimace.

"When I was young, I used to ask my neighbors if there were any jobs I could do for them to earn some extra money," Dit told L'il Dobber.

"Who's going to pay me sixteen dollars to do work for them?" asked L'il Dobber.

"Not any one person," said Dit. "You'll have to do small jobs for a few of them."

L'il Dobber watched his dad reach for a second helping of liver. *A second helping?!*

"What if everyone says no?" he asked.

"You won't know until you ask them," his mom pointed out.

L'il Dobber stirred rice around his plate

and thought for a moment. Then he said, "There are a lot of leaves lying around the street. Maybe people are tired of raking them."

"Good idea," said his dad. "After school tomorrow you can offer to rake some of the neighbors' yards."

"For just a dollar or two each," reminded his mother.

L'il Dobber nodded. "I hope they say yes!"

L'il Dobber loved basketball so much that he was actually looking forward to cleaning up his neighbors' yards.

Chapter 9
Job Search

As he slowly walked up to Mr. Palmer's house the next afternoon, L'il Dobber made sure his feet didn't even come close to stepping on the grass. He had worked up the courage to start his job searching here. After all, scrambling away from Mr. Palmer was what had gotten his ball run over in the first place. He felt like maybe Mr. Palmer owed him.

Tap, tap, tap. L'il Dobber knocked lightly on the metal screen door. The main door was open and he could hear a TV inside, but no one answered.

Boom, boom, boom. L'il Dobber knocked harder. He was already this close, and he was going to make it worthwhile.

"What?!" came an angry yell from inside.

Actually, maybe this isn't a good place to start, thought L'il Dobber. He looked over at his own house, wondering if he could get back there before Mr. Palmer saw him. Nope.

"What?!" demanded Mr. Palmer coming toward the front door.

"Hi, Mr. Palmer!" L'il Dobber tried to sound cheerful.

Mr. Palmer didn't say "hi" back, so L'il Dobber continued with the speech he had planned.

"I was wondering if you would like some help with your yard work." L'il Dobber paused. "I will rake your leaves for two dollars," he announced.

"No, thank you. You already ruined my flowers," Mr. Palmer said flatly.

"That was an accident," replied L'il Dobber. "I'm good at raking leaves."

"I've never needed anyone to help me with my yard. Or with anything else for that matter," Mr. Palmer told him.

L'il Dobber sighed. *So much for my first try at finding a job.*

Other neighbors were much more excited about L'il Dobber's plan to earn money for a new basketball. Over the next week, the Abels, the Stephens, and Mrs. Lester paid him two dollars each for raking leaves. Plus, Mrs. Lester paid him two dollars and fifty cents more for putting a bunch of old books into boxes.

His hardest-earned two dollars had been clearing out the Whitleys' flower bed. He felt like he had weeded a whole farm that afternoon. On his chart, he colored in those two sections extra dark. And he used orange and blue — the colors of his favorite team, the New York Knicks.

L'il Dobber was working hard. Every night he counted his money, colored his chart, and re-hid his lockbox and key. Then he instantly fell asleep, dreaming about shooting hoops with his new ball.

Chapter 10
Five More Dollars

L'il Dobber, Joe, Gan, and Sam crouched around the chalk target they had drawn on L'il Dobber's driveway. They were competing to see who could roll a tennis ball closest to the center. It was the first afternoon in a week that L'il Dobber could spend with his friends.

"I only need five more dollars," L'il Dobber announced happily.

"Wow. That's it?" asked Gan.

"That's great!" exclaimed Joe. He rolled his tennis ball and knocked Sam's ball out of the circle.

"I just have to find a way to earn it," L'il

Dobber said. "My mom and dad have run out of extra jobs I can do, and I've raked leaves at every house from here to the next corner. Except, of course, for the Grouch."

"He was probably afraid to let you go near his lawn," said Gan. "It seems like he treats his yard better than he treats his neighbors!"

Sam concentrated on rolling her tennis ball back onto the target and then asked L'il Dobber, "What about your allowance?"

L'il Dobber shrugged. "I guess. But that's three weeks worth of allowance to wait for."

"Five more dollars, huh?" said Joe. "Maybe you'll find it on the street."

"Doubt it," replied L'il Dobber. "Of all the money I've saved so far, I only found fifty cents of it on the street."

Gan's tennis ball was closest to the center. They all grabbed the balls and took turns trying again.

"Maybe you'll win it," Gan suggested excitedly.

"How would I win five dollars?" L'il Dobber asked Gan.

"I don't know that part," admitted Gan. "I just thought it would be exciting."

"Well, when I do get my new basketball, I'm keeping it far away from the Grouch," L'il Dobber said. He nodded across the driveway. "I feel like he's a referee watching every move I make."

Joe laughed. "I'm surprised he doesn't jump out and blow a whistle every time you get close to his house," he joked.

"And scream, 'Out of bounds!' at me," yelled L'il Dobber, waving his arms in the air.

That thought made them all crack up.

From his porch a few days later, L'il Dobber saw Mr. Abel, who lived on the other side of Mr. Palmer, put a stack of newspapers by the curb for the recycling truck. Then Mr. Abel got in his car and drove away.

The newspapers were not weighted down or tied up with string, and L'il Dobber watched every car that sped past blow more of them into the air. The papers all landed on Mr. Palmer's yard.

So that's how Mr. Palmer's yard got covered in newspapers the other day! L'il Dobber figured out.

Then L'il Dobber had another thought. *He's going to blame me for this mess.*

Mr. Palmer's front door was shut so L'il Dobber figured he wasn't home. He walked over to Mr. Palmer's yard. *Maybe I can pick up the newspapers before he gets home. If he doesn't see them, he can't blame me.*

L'il Dobber opened the gate and hurried to grab all the papers. Rushing around the yard, he didn't see Mr. Palmer walking down the street. He jumped when Mr. Palmer grunted "hmpf" right behind him.

With his hands full of papers, L'il Dobber tried to explain why he was there. "Umm, the Abels' newspapers blew all over your yard. I was just picking them up. I'll leave now."

Mr. Palmer stood there with his arms crossed. So L'il Dobber dropped the newspapers and went back to his porch.

Instead of cleaning up the newspapers littered all over his yard, Mr. Palmer walked into his house. And then came right back out.

"L'il Dobber!" yelled Mr. Palmer. "Come over here!"

L'il Dobber stared at him.

"It's OK," said Mr. Palmer without yelling.

L'il Dobber walked slowly from his house over to his neighbor's yard and then to where Mr. Palmer stood on his front walkway.

Mr. Palmer held out a five-dollar bill. "Here you go, L'il Dobber," he said.

Once again, L'il Dobber was tongue-tied. He didn't know if he was more surprised at the money or that Mr. Palmer was calling him by his nickname.

"I heard you talking to your friends in the driveway," said Mr. Palmer, and his face cracked into a smile. An actual smile.

"I know you need five more dollars for your basketball, so here you go," he continued. "I appreciate your help trying to clean up all these papers — and I'm sorry I blamed you before. It's a little bit my fault that your ball got run over in the first place."

L'il Dobber raised his eyebrows.

"I saw you running away from me," Mr. Palmer explained.

Then he actually started to laugh a little bit. "I never meant to become the neighborhood grouch," he said, chuckling.

L'il Dobber's eyes widened.

"I heard you say that to your friends, too," Mr. Palmer explained.

"Sorry," said L'il Dobber, embarrassed.

Mr. Palmer shrugged. "I deserve it sometimes. Maybe it's true that I treat my yard better than I treat some people."

Mr. Palmer put the five dollars in L'il Dobber's hand. "I need to learn to let people help me sometimes, too," he said, pointing to all the newspapers on his lawn.

"I was really just doing it so you wouldn't get mad at me," L'il Dobber admitted.

"Well, for whatever reason, I appreciate it," Mr. Palmer said. "Now keep off the grass on your way home," he said with the smile that L'il Dobber wasn't sure he would ever get used to seeing. "I'll be listening for that new basketball thumping on the driveway."

L'il Dobber nodded and started toward his house. Halfway home L'il Dobber realized he had forgotten to say "thank you," and turned back. Mr. Palmer was hurrying around picking up the newspapers.

L'il Dobber stuffed the five-dollar bill into his pocket and walked back over to Mr. Palmer's house. He began picking up newspapers right alongside his neighbor.

"Thank you," said L'il Dobber as he worked.

"You, too," replied Mr. Palmer, nodding at the papers in L'il Dobber's hand.

"You're welcome," said L'il Dobber. Then he tried something he'd never tried before. L'il Dobber smiled his first smile ever at Mr. Palmer.

About the Authors

Bob Lanier is a basketball legend and a member of the Basketball Hall of Fame. A graduate of St. Bonaventure University, he has been hailed as much for his work in the community as for his play on the court. Winner of numerous awards and honors, he currently serves as Special Assistant to NBA Commissioner David Stern and as Captain of the NBA's All-Star Reading Team.

Like L'il Dobber, Bob has faced life's challenges head-on with a positive attitude and a never-ending belief in the power and value of reading and education.

Bob and his wife, Rose, have eight children and reside in Scottsdale, Arizona.

Heather Goodyear started creative writing in the first grade, with poems she wrote on scraps of paper. Her teacher gave her a blank notebook and said, "Be sure to let me know when you publish your first book." Hey L'il D! is her first series.

Sports were an important part of Heather's childhood in Michigan. As the only girl in a close family with two brothers, she learned early to hold her own in living room wrestling matches, driveway basketball contests, and family football games.

Heather says that this love of sports and her classroom experience as a teacher, makes Hey L'il D! especially fun for her to write.

Heather lives in Arizona with her husband, Chris, and their three young children.